The Wonderful Wizard of Oz
Toki Pona edition

I0642997

translated by Sonja Lang
illustrated by Evan Dahm

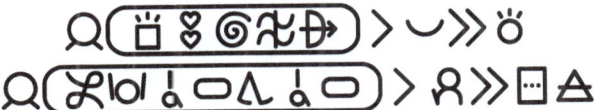

Work Group

Written in English by L. Frank Baum.
Translated to Toki Pona by Sonja Lang.
Illustrated by Evan Dahm (*rice-boy.com*).
Proofread by jan Kekan San, jan Pensa, jan Asiku, jan Sepulon and jan Polijan.
nasin nanpa font by Ethan.
With help from jan Ke Tami, Lipamanka and Emmanuelle Richard.
Published by Sonja Lang.

ISBN: 978-0-9782923-7-9

⁒ ◻ Book Parts

SS 101

⊙✧1) SSⓦLΛ◎>𝘈
△ⓦ>⊹ㄴL△˘
Ω⊕+Ω⟫>Λ☞
⊣Ω⟨△⟩>ᘜ×⟫⊙>KXΛ△ㄴ
⊙˘) SSⓦ>Λ⟫△Λᡰᢆ
Ω⟨△⟩+ᔆᵖ⟨ᵒ̈⟩>⊹�△

The Strong Wind

A little girl named Dorothy did not have two parents. But Dorothy had other people in the parental group. A person called Em and a person called Henry were like parents to Dorothy. They all stayed in a house in the land called Kansas. This land was wheat land and was not colourful and did not have many people or many things. Every sun period, all the people worked a lot in the land of no entertainment. In their small house, there was a lot of unpleasant furniture. Only a mammal named Toto gave feelings of fun to Dorothy.

On one sun period, a powerful wind of circular movement came. A strong room was located under the small house. Em and Henry went to it. But Dorothy did not have time and could not go to the lower room. In a short time, the strong wind moved the house towards the sky. Dorothy and Toto were located inside the house.

ㅴㄴㄴㅇ◎ㅈᴧ＞ᴧㅴㄴㄴΩ⌂
ㅴㄴ＞♡△＞ᴧ◉

ω#1ㄴΩ⌂＞↓
ᵒ◦ᴧ⊕♀ㅂ↓＝∞∸☉∸
◎ᴧㄴ⊕✳＞ᵓ》ᵒ
「↓＞⊕◦∀♀
　◦ꝶ》ᵕᵔΩ◦∀♀ㄴᴧ◉∸⊕⌂ㄴ♡爻
　◦ᴧ∸↑ㄴ♡爻」
◎ᴧ＞♀》ᵓ◉ㄴΩ⌂
♀↓＞ᵓ》⊟＞ᴧ》Ω⌂₩ᴧ◉
◎ᴧ＞ᴧ✕
Ω⌂＞ㅛ》ᴧ∀∸◡ㄴ¿ᵒ♥ᵒ♥
Ω˅|||⊙＞ᵒ》「ᴧ◡」

Knowledge of the Little Munchkin People

Fortunately, the house went down in a colourful distant land of beauty. In this land, the person called Dorothy managed to talk to many little people called Munchkins and talked to the Powerful Woman of the Cold Land.

Dorothy came to know this: When the house came down, it killed the Evil Powerful Woman of the Sun's Arrival. This woman cruelly ruled the group called Munchkins in the past. At this time, the Munchkins became fully capable and felt good. The Good Powerful Woman of the Cold Land gave this knowledge: This land has good powerful women and evil powerful women. Dorothy became a powerful person in the feelings of the Munchkins because of this: She killed an evil person.

The foot clothing of the Evil Powerful Woman became the foot clothing of Dorothy. The foot clothing was white metal and was strangely powerful. The number one desire of Dorothy was this: She should go to the land called Kansas again. The Powerful Woman of the Cold Land gave knowledge: "This is the land called Oz. Seek help from the Person of Strange Powers Called Oz in the Residential Land of the Blue-Green Mineral. Go on the road of yellow stones." The powerful woman applied her mouth to the upper part of Dorothy's head. This kiss gave a mark and protected Dorothy using strange powers. The powerful woman went away. Dorothy began the long travel at the side of the mammal called Toto. The many little people called Munchkins said "safe travels".

↑⚺⟩Ω⌂⟩⟩⋏⊙≫⯄∟⤬⅌
⌐⟩⸱◌⸱⊕⟫
◎⟩⯄↓⟩⚮⟫⟩⟩⎺˘⹀Ω
Ω⌂⟩⟩⟩⟩⟩ΩL⤬⅌⌒◖

⌐ρ♡⌒⌒↓
   ⨀ӨΡ⟩⌒⟫
   Ρ⨆⚮⟫⨀Ө⸱⌐
Ω⌂⟩⟩♡⟫⌒⌐
⌐⸱⟩⋏⸱⨆Ρ
   ΡⳆ⊕⌂L♡⚺
   ΡⳆ⟫↓
   ⊕↓⟩Ω⸱⟩▽⟩L⨆⚮⟩Ϗ⸚⟫⨀Ө⋏ϸ⌐

The Person of Bird Removal

In the land called Oz, the person called Dorothy wanted to go to the Residential Land of the Blue-Green Mineral. She had an unsoiled cute garment and the metal footwear of strange powers. At the side of the mammal named Toto, Dorothy began the travel on the road of yellow stones. During the travel, she saw good-looking lands and the strange blue-green houses of the group called Munchkins. These little people loved Dorothy because of her powerful deed.

When the dark time was near, many little people called Munchkins said "welcome" to Dorothy. They felt good and played because of this: They are capable of everything because of the end of the rule of the evil woman. "Eat greatly. You and the cute mammal should rest in our house during the dark time." Dorothy slept pleasantly. At the arrival of the sun, Dorothy departed.

On the yellow road, Dorothy came to see a device of bird removal. It was located on a pole on wheat land. Strangely, this device had a spirit and spoke like a person. Dorothy removed the Person of Bird Removal from the pole.

"I feel bad because of this: My head innards are stalks of grain. I want to have a real head organ." Dorothy felt his problem. "Come at my side. I am going to the Residential Land of the Blue-Green Mineral. I want this: In this land, the Person of Strange Powers Called Oz can give a head organ to you."

Plant Land

The person called Dorothy and the Person of Bird Removal and the mammal called Toto walked on the yellow road. At this time, the road was located inside a large plant land. There were many mushrooms.

The dark time came. Dorothy's group sought a rest house. The Person of Bird Removal could see well in the darkness and managed to see a small house. In this context, Dorothy could sleep.

At no time, the Person of Bird Removal needed rest. During the sleep time of Dorothy, the Person of Bird Removal stayed and looked and wanted this: May a bad thing not happen. He was a good companion.

ՈᏇᒪ፨Ψ

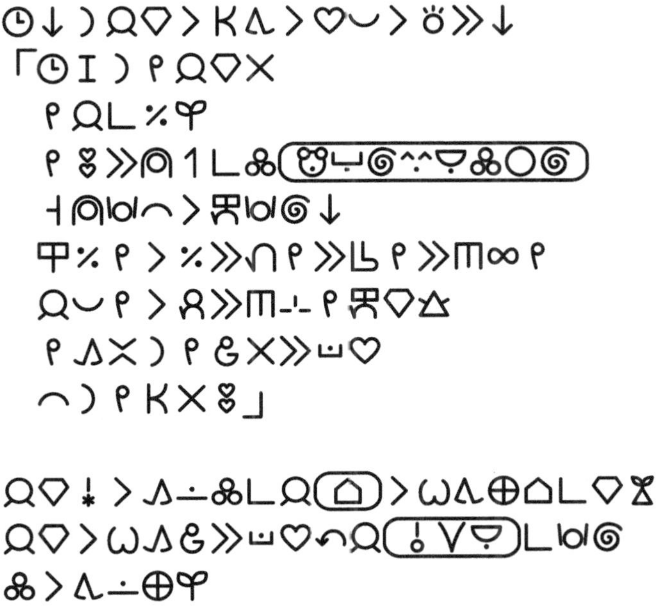

⊙↓)Ω♡>ΚΛ>♡◡>ö≫↓
⌐⊙I)ρΩ♡✕
  ρΩL⁒Ψ
  ρ⧈≫ⴹ1Lꝸ(🙂ⴤ◉⌃⌄▽ꝸ◯◉)
  ⊣ⴲ囘⌒>🐦囘◉↓
  中⁒ρ>⁒≫∩ρ≫Ⴑρ≫Ⅲ∞ρ
  Ω◡ρ>ꝝ≫Ⅲ⌐'- ρ🐦♡⚠
  ρⴠ✕)ρⴀ✕≫⊡♡
  ⌒)ρΚ✕⧈」

Ω♡⁑>ⴠ÷ꝸLΩ(⌂)>ⵠⴠ⊕⌂L♡⚥
Ω♡>ⵠⴠⴀ≫⊡♡⤵Ω(⁞∨▽)L囘◉
ꝸ>ⴠ÷⊕Ψ

The Metal Person of Plant Cutting

Again, Dorothy and the Person of Bird Removal and the mammal called Toto travelled. The group came to see a metal person. But reddish damage was eating the metal body of this person. Because of this, the Metal Person could not move. As his mouth was not open, he could only make vocalizations of feeling bad. Dorothy used some liquid of tool improvement on the body of the Metal Person.

At this time, the Metal Person could move and felt good and said this: "In the past, I was not a metal person. I was a person of plant cutting. I loved one woman of the group called Munchkins. But an Evil Powerful Woman used these strange powers: My cutting tool cut my arms and my legs and my entire body. A good person made my new body using white metal. As I became different, I did not have an organ of emotion. Unfortunately, I could not love."

The Metal Person as well came in Dorothy's group and wanted to go to the Residential Land of the Blue-Green Mineral. The Metal Person wanted to successfully have an organ of emotion from the Person of Strange Powers Called Oz. The group walked in the plant land.

The Strong Beast of Fearful Feelings

The group walked on the road of yellow stones. At this time, a strong beast came and tried to attack the group.

But the Strong Beast did not attack and felt afraid. "I am large. Other people can feel afraid of me. But I too feel afraid. I want to feel confident."

The person called Dorothy felt the problem of the large Beast and welcomed him in the travel group. The Beast wanted to successfully have feelings of confidence from the Person of Strange Powers Called Oz.

On the yellow road, the Metal Person walked erroneously and kicked a bug. The Metal Person felt very bad. "I do not want to harm a living being. In the future, I will be able to have an organ of emotion. This should improve my feelings and intentions of action."

⊕LUV

&⌣⟩ഡ⋏⊕⌂∟♡⅄) ⌐⟩⋏⊙≫UV∸↑
⌒)⌐⟩ΚΧ⋏⌐⋅ΧLUV
┼⇲⅃⌃∟♡⅃Χ⟩ΚΛ⌐⟩ΚΛ⌐⋅Χ
Ω1⟩⋏∸⟮⇲)⇲⅃⌃⟩⋏≫⌐
⇲⟩⋏≫Ω&∞∸↑=

⌒Χ⟩⋏
⊕Ϙ↓)⇲⌇⋙Ⅲ⟩∸
◠⌐⟩⇲⌒⟨&↓⅄⌒⋏↓⟩
⊓∟⇲⟨&⟩⟩=⇲V
⊖⌐⟩=⇲⅏

The Land of the Deep Holes

While the good group wanted to go to the Residential Land of the Blue-Green Mineral, they came to see a deep hole in the road. Unfortunately, they could not go to the other side of the large hole. But the Strong Beast of Not Feeling Confident could move upwards and could go to the other side. When one person became located on the Beast's back, the Strong Beast moved them. The Beast transported all group persons in the same way.

Another problem came. In this plant land, there were many monstrous animals. Their name was the evil animals called Kalidahs. The body of the Kalidahs was like a large animal. Their head was like a predatory animal.

The group of good people went away from the many monsters called Kalidahs, but there was a second deep hole. The Metal Person cut a large plant. The group could use this large trunk like a passage located above the large hole. The group went to the other side. But many Kalidahs kept coming. In a short time, the Metal Person cut the large plant. The monsters went down.

This time, the group arrived at a large line of water. The Metal Person cut some plants and made an aquatic moving platform and put it on the water. All the people came onto the moving platform. Unfortunately, the strength of the water moved the platform. The platform was very far from the good road of yellow stones. The Strong Beast of Fearful Feelings moved in the water and managed to hold the platform and moved the platform to the land.

ⱵℙⱯ⚹⟩ℙ⟩ⵝⵔ
Ⱳⵔ⟩ⱯⱵ⟩Ⴘ⟩⟩Ⴘ⟩Κⵝℬ⟩⟩ⵔ
⌢⟩ℙⱯ⟩ⵝⵔⵥ⊕ᒪⵕⵤ

Ⲩⵝⵝ⟩ⵝⵝ⟩⟩ℛ◻︎ⵝ⊕ᒪⵕⵝⵝ⊕⌣
ⵔⵝⵝ⟩ⵝ
◉⟩ⵝⵔⵔ

The Land of the Sleep Plants

The group wanted to travel at length, but there was a new problem. In this land, there were many red plants. Their pleasant air could cause a person to sleep. For a long time, the person called Dorothy and the small mammal called Toto consumed the air and became asleep. The Person of Bird Removal and the Metal Person of Plant Cutting were mechanical. The sleep plants could not cause them to sleep. The two of them used their arms and held Dorothy and Toto.

But the large Beast too was an animal and became asleep. As his body was very large, the two mechanical ones could not carry him. Unfortunately, the large Beast stayed asleep in the land of the red plants.

The two mechanical ones moved Dorothy away from the land of the sleep plants and to a good land. The two of them waited. The girl came from sleep.

The Ruling Small Mammal

At this time, the person named Dorothy and her group came to see a small mammal. Unfortunately, a predatory animal with red eyes was present and wanted to eat the small mammal. The Metal Person defeated the evil predatory animal and protected the small mammal. Because of this, the small mammal felt good and said this: "I want to give help to your group. I rule all small mammals." The Person of Bird Removal said this: "A friendly large Beast still sleeps in the land of the red plants. All your small mammals should give help."

The ruling small mammal caused all small mammals to arrive. They were so very many and brought many small ropes. The Metal Person built a moving platform with many wheels. All the small mammals used many ropes and used the transportation device and could move the sleeping large Beast from the land of the sleep plants. Since the small mammals used little time, they did not sleep. All was well.

The ruling small mammal gave a musical instrument to Dorothy. The group spoke to the ruling small mammal: "You are very good. At this time, we are leaving." The group went to the Residential Land of the Blue-Green Mineral.

The Protective Person of the Large Wall

Finally, the group came upon a large wall of mineral. This wall of mineral was located at the boundary of the residential land. As the road of the yellow stones ended, there was a large door of blue-green mineral.

The group used the noise device of the large door. The Protective Person of the Large Wall came and listened: "Oh, hello! We want to talk to the important person called Oz." The eyes of the protective person became big. "Oz is a scary person of strange powers. Few people want to talk to him. I can lead you to Oz. But the blue-green minerals of the city are intensely shiny and can damage your eyes, so please use these eye instruments." All the people and all the animals received eye instruments. The group went to the area inside the blue-green residential land. The Protective Person led the group.

⊕⌂L♡✄

⊕⌂ > V⌀� > ◇⌀⌀ ↓

⌂∞ > ♡✄

Ω∞L⊕⌂ > ↻ >> ⊟✄
       > ⊙ >> ஃLΩ ⌂✄ω⊕˜○
       > ⊙X >> Ω⋅⋅ ↓

⊚) ∞ > ✄

Ψ⋀+≈♡ > ✄

⊥✄⋮ > ⊙⊙ >> ◎♀✄

Ω > ⊙ >> ஃLΩ⌣⋀⌂▽LΩ ⊙V♡

ΩX > ⋅⋅

⌣✄ > ⋅⋅⊹L⊙⌐

ΩX > ⊙ >> ↓

「Ω1⊣ > KΛ⋅⋅⊦LΩ ⊙ ⋅⋅⊙1
    ஃ > KXΛ⋅⋅⊙=
     ⋮Λ⋅⋅⌂↓」

⌂LΩ ⌂ > ↻ >> π⊸✄

⊙♢⅄)Ω⬡>⅄ᘓ》Ⱶ🗲>Ⲕ⅄Ω|ol(ᵔ)
ᕲ>⅄ᵚ⌐⌂V

|ol)ϴV(ᵔ)⌐ⲘX>∸
  ⌐ᖰΩV(ᵔ)ᓭ
    ᖰⱲn̈》⌣⅄ᕲ
    ᖰⲔ⅄》ᕲ⅄⊕(Ⴤᖯ↓═∞)
    ⊦#1)ᕲᓭᖯ》⊙|ol⌒⌐♢I⌟
Ω⬡>♡ⱮⱮⱮ
ᕲ>ⲔXⲔ↓

⊙↓)ΩLメⅇ>ΚΛΩ⊡
⊙)Ω⊡>=ⴖL◡⊙
Γρｋ◌̈》⊖
⊣b¡↵》》◍◌↶Γ

I) ꝘⱱⱭᒻ♡ⱱᑊX>⅄Ω⬭

☉) Ω⬭)><=⸾⸾∨

ꜱ P ⸚≫♡ⱱⱭ ꝑ
⼁ ꝑ ⼂ ⼂≫Ꙙ⌐

Ω∞ꙮ>Ɛ≫ꙍꞳ=
☉⚭⅄)ꙮ>⅄

Residential Land of the Blue-Green Mineral

The residential land was intensely large and was so intensely bright. All houses were of blue-green mineral. All people of the city had blue-green clothing and looked at Dorothy's group and did not know these new people. Strangely, everything was blue-green. The transportation devices and the fruit juice were blue-green. Even a blue-green bird gave a blue-green parental oval.

Somebody led the group of good people to the large house of the person named Oz. A battle person was present. Blue-green hair was at the lower part of his head. The battle person said this: "Only one person can come in front of Oz at one time. The group cannot come at the same time. Please wait in this building." Dorothy's room had a blue-green piece of furniture for sleeping.

On the next sun period, Dorothy received blue-green clothing and could go to the Mighty Oz. She went to the inside of a large room.

Powerfully, a large head with no body called Oz was present. "I am the important person named Oz! I want to give help to you. I can transport you to the land called Kansas. But first, you must defeat the Evil Powerful Woman of the Ending Sun." Dorothy felt afraid. Could she do this?

At this time, the Person of Bird Removal could go to Oz. Visually, Oz was like a good-looking woman. "I can give a head organ. But you must defeat the Evil Powerful Woman."

Similarly, the Metal Person of Plant Cutting went to Oz. Visually, Oz was like a monstrous animal. "Defeat the Evil Powerful Woman, and then I will put a heart inside you."

Finally, the Strong Beast of Not Feeling Confident went to Oz. Visually, Oz was like a large fire. "I will give feelings of confidence to you. But you must defeat the Evil Powerful Woman."

All people of the group had the same duty to act. On the coming sun period, the group departed.

⋒ⅼⅾ∧ㄴ◇Ⅰ

⅘⟩∧⊕ㄴ⋒ⅼⅾ∧⟩⋒∧⟩Ⅼ⊙》⌐⋐⊞Ⴑ⊙ㄴⅼⅾ◎
⋒ⅼⅾ∧⟩ŏ∧⩗⊕Ⅲ
「¦⤬》⅘ㄴ☡（⌂⅛ⱳ⩗⌒⌒〇）」
┤☡♡ㄴ⤬Ψ⟩ŏ⊞Ⴑ⤬
⋄⟩ㄴ》⩚⤬⟩∧⟩⅘ㄴ☡◡

⊙↓⃩)ᗞ⌒∟⅊◎>⋏⋗⋗⋏⧄Ⅲ
「⸕𝗑」
┤Ω∟⤬⋏>ö⤬⋗⋗⋏
⸕>⸕ᗗ⋗⋗ᗞ⸕
⋏𝗑>♡ᾳ>∟𝗑

⊙↓⟩⧣☒⛰>♫
「⸸✕」
⊦⅋ᒐᑫꝰ>ᛜⅢ⅍⊟↶ᑫᒐ✕⍀⇉Ⅲᕠ
↓⟩⧣✕>Ʞ✕⧇≫ᑫꝰ

ᑎᗷᗩᐯᗰᖉ
ᖎᐯᐳᕮ♓ᗝᒪᗷᖑᐳᐱᐱᐳᑫᗝᕫ

⯂⯅Ⅲ⟩⅊⟫ႷⳐⵝ⅄⟩⟫Ⴗ♡Ⳑⵝ⚲

Ⴍ∥↓⟩⟩ⵝ

⯂⯅⟩⥤ᔎ⟩⅊⟫⯂ᓙႷⳐ♡ᓙ⨯⟩ⵜ⟫ᕽ⋏⋒ᓙᓙᔎ

⊙Ⅰ⟩⋒ᓙᔎᨓႷ⊕⚹⟩▽⟫Ⴍ⌂⟩ⵜ⟫⊟⋏⊹⛫⊙ᕽ

ᔎ↓⟩⋒ᓙᔎ⟩Ⲕ⨯⊞⟫Ⴍ⌂

✝⯂⯅⟩⋏⟫Ⴍ⌂⋏⌂ᓙႷ⋒ᔎ

△∨⎵⍀Ω⌂⟩∧Ω५Lⵡ✕
⋒⌒⟩☉≫ᕈ
「¡ꓤ≫ⴑꝒ
 ✕⎵Ꝓ✕≫Ꮾ⍦ⵔ Ꝓ∟✕≋」
Ω⌂⟩♡⌒

⋒ᑭ⌒⟩ⵡᏰ≫ᕗ∟∟∟♡△⌒Ω⌂
ᕈ⟩ᨆ≫ⵔ♡⸚ᴛᴛ५
ᔕᑭᏓ⎵Ω⌂⟩Ҟ✕☉≫ⵔ⟩∧ᛯ⟩∧५
⤊↓⎵⋒⌒⟩ᕗ≫ᕗ∟1

Q⌂〉♡✕〉ⁿ◔ˇ⬠⟩⟩≈⋏⬠◔⬠⌒
↓)⬠⌒〉ⁿ◔⬠L♡⌒
Γ⌒å
  ≈〉⬚⟩⟩ρΓ⌐
ⲘL⬠⌒〉⋏≈

☉↓)⬠⌒〉⊗
ⱺ⌒〉I
q⌂+☙↤〉KΛ
q⌂〉ꝍ∹⟩⟩丹Ⱡ

☙Lq◡〉♡◡
↤¡Ꝛ⟩⟩?
☉Λ)q◔⟨¡VȢ⟩¡ⁿ⟩⟩ꞷV↤

The Evil Powerful Woman of the Ending Sun

As the group went to the land of the Evil Powerful Woman, the Evil Woman could watch them using an observation device of strange powers. The Evil Powerful Woman spoke to many predatory animals: "Attack Dorothy's group." But the Metal Person of Plant Cutting knew how to use a cutting tool. He defeated the attacking animals and defended the group of good people.

This time, the Evil Woman of Strange Powers caused many black birds to arrive. "Attack!" But the Person of Bird Removal knew how to get rid of birds. He raised his arms. The attacking birds felt afraid and went away.

This time, yellow and black insects arrived. "Attack!" But the group of good people used the internal stalks of grain from the Person of Bird Removal on their skin. In this context, the attacking insects could not harm the good people.

The Evil Powerful Woman felt bad. She used a head garment of strange powers and summoned the winged humanlike beasts.

Many winged beasts seized the Person of Bird Removal and the Metal Person of Plant Cutting. These two people were gone. The winged beasts used a rope and seized the Strong Beast of Not Feeling Confident and gave him to the Evil Powerful Woman.

In the past, the Good Powerful Woman of the Cold Land applied her mouth to Dorothy and gave a protective mark on her upper head. Because of this, the Evil Powerful Woman could not harm

Dorothy. But the winged beasts transported Dorothy to the strong house of the Evil Woman.

In the large building, Dorothy became an unwilling subservient person. The Evil Woman controlled her. "Do my will. Otherwise, I will strike you with my stick of water repelling." Dorothy felt bad.

The Evil Powerful Woman wanted to have the footwear of white metal from Dorothy. She placed a metal bar on the lower surface. Due to strange powers, Dorothy could not see the bar and moved erroneously and moved downward. In this way, the Evil Woman stole one item of footwear.

Dorothy felt aggressive and strongly put water towards the Evil Powerful Woman. In this context, the Evil Woman spoke loudly with pain: "How bad! Water harms me." The body of the Evil Woman became liquid.

At this moment, the Evil Woman was dead. The evil control was finished. Dorothy and her group could go. Dorothy got back the footwear.

The group of good people felt good. What should they do? In the future, the powerful person called Oz should grant their big wishes.

⊙↓)⅋>ωⁿ»⌣⋏Ω⅃╳ᴭ
⅋>⋏⊙»⊟⊸⸱⊹♇∨
⅋>ⁿ»⌣≽⸱⌐⸱⊸⌐⊸
⊙↓)Ω⅃╳ᴭ>♡⌣∞
Ω∞⅋>⌣>1⸱⌐>♡⌣⸱△|0|

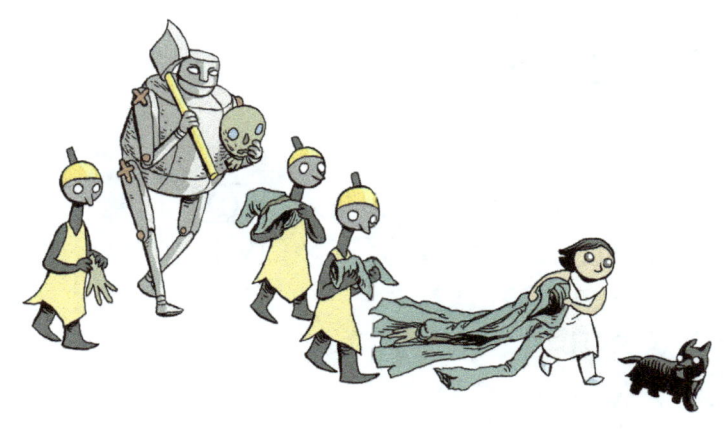

†Ω⌂)>⋏♡»╳⅃ᵠ⊕⊤⊙
⌐ℙωⅠ⊕♇↳↓≡∞
Ω⸱⸱∨ᵠ⸱ⁿ»⌣⋏ℙ∞⌐
Ω♡>ω»♡
Ω⅃╳ᴭ>ω»⌐ö
᠁ℙ∨>ω»♡|0|
ω|0|)⅋⸱⋏⊕⌂⅃♡⅊⸱♢⋏

⊣⅋ⓌⓌ〉⅋ⵊⵊⵊ》Ω∟▽△
⌈⸫∧⸭⸜∟ℙⵊⵊⵊ
  ⸫⊖》ℙⵊⵊⵊ⌋
⊣⅋∟Ω⌣〉ⱳ△⟩Ω▽〉K✕⊖⸚⊙↓

⅋Ⓦ〉♡⌣⟩
ⴰ〉ⵚ》ⵛ⊖∟▽⅋∆ℙⓄ⅋ⵚ⅋∆ℙⱽ
  〉ⵚ》ⵛ∩∟▽⊖∆Ω⌂
  〉ⵚ⊖∟▽⅋∆Ω∟✕⌖
  〉ⵚ》ⵤⵛ∟≈Ψ∆Ω▽
⌈∆⌣⌋

Ω⌂〉∆⅋》⊟⊖∟▽⅋∩Θⴰ⊗
⌈ℙⵝ✕》ⴱⓈⴰ⊣ⴰ〉⌣⊙⌋
⅋〉∆

The Giving of All Possibilities

The Evil Powerful Woman was gone for all of time. The Strong Beast of Not Feeling Confident was located in a holding container. The person named Dorothy opened the container. The two of them were together and felt good. In the building of the Evil Woman, there were many subservient people with yellow clothing called Winkies. At this time, the group called Winkies were capable of everything and felt good. There was a large amusement time.

Dorothy felt the absence of the other good people and grouped together many Winkies. They left and wanted to manage to see the Person of Bird Removal and the Metal Person of Plant Cutting. First, the group successfully saw the Metal Person. Reddish damage consumed his body. The Winkies moved him to a yellow strong building. In this buliding, many Winkies knew how to repair white metal and repaired him. The Metal Person felt good again.

This time, the group wanted to give help to the Person of Bird Removal. The group managed to see his clothing on a large plant. The group put new stalks of grain inside him. At this time, the Person of Bird Removal felt completely good. All people of the group were well and united again and felt good in the strong building.

But Dorothy still felt the absence of the caretaker named Em. "I want to go to the land called Kansas. The person called Oz should give help to us all." The Metal Person wanted a heart. The Person of Bird Removal wanted an organ of knowledge. The large Beast wanted feelings of confidence. With strong desire, the group should go to the Residential Land of the Blue-Green Mineral during the coming sun.

But the Winkies loved the Person of White Metal a lot. "Stay with us. Lead us." But the group of friends wanted to go, and so the Metal Person could not lead at this time.

As the Winkies felt good, they gave head adornments of yellow metal to the mammal called Toto and to the large Beast, gave a hand adornment of valuable gems to Dorothy, gave a rod of yellow metal to the Person of Bird Removal, and gave a decorative container of tool liquid to the Metal Person. "Safe travels."

Dorothy came to have the headdress of yellow metal from the dead Evil Woman. "I do not know its strange powers, but it is visually good." The group left.

ꝏꝎꝎꝏ

ꝏꝏꝎꝏꝎꝏꝏꝎꝏꝎꝏ
ꝏꝏꝏꝏ
ꝏꝏꝏꝏꝏꝏꝏꝏꝏꝏꝏ
「ꝏꝏꝏꝏꝏꝏ
　ꝏꝏ」

ꝏꝏꝏꝏꝏꝏꝏꝏꝏꝏꝏ
ꝏ(ꝏꝏꝏꝏꝏꝏ)ꝏꝏꝏꝏꝏꝏꝏꝏꝏ
「ꝏꝏꝏꝏꝏ
　ꝏꝏꝏꝏ」

ꝏꝏꝏꝏ(ꝏ)ꝏꝏꝏꝏꝏꝏꝏꝏ
ꝏꝏꝏꝏꝏꝏꝏ
「ꝏꝏꝏꝏꝏꝏꝏꝏ
　ꝏꝏꝏꝏꝏ」

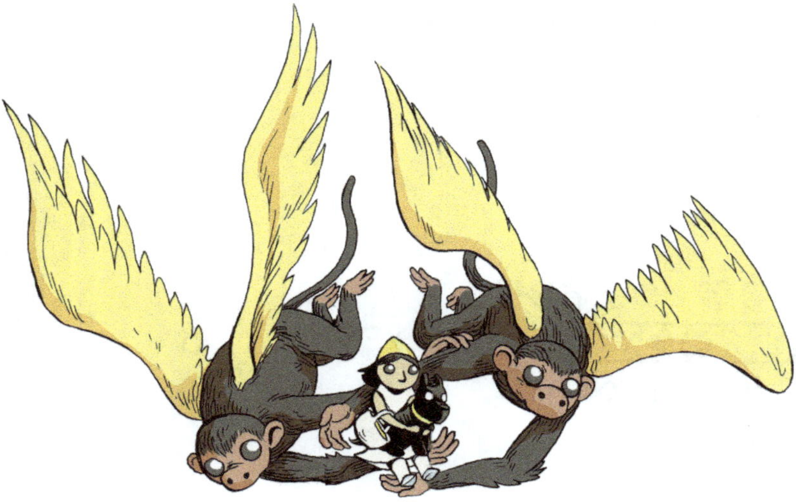

The Winged Humanlike Beasts

The group of good people wanted to go to the Residential Land of the Blue-Green Mineral. But there was no path. The Person of Bird Removal and the Metal Person of Plant Cutting felt bad. "We cannot go to the city. How bad!"

In the past, the ruling small mammal gave a musical instrument. The person named Dorothy caused it to make a sound, and then the small mammals arrived and spoke. "Use the headdress of strange powers. Look inside it."

Inside the article of clothing, Dorothy saw powerful words and recited them. This caused the winged humanlike beasts to come. "We obey the person with the headdress. State your desire." "Transport us to the Residential Land of the Blue-Green Mineral." Using strong arms, the winged beasts did this.

&Ⴑ♀(⌂ะ꒼ധꝶ∴◯)〉⅄⌐⌐∵⊕⌂Ⴑ♡⦂
　　　　　　　〉ധ≫◡ꞑ♀∨(¡V♀)
♀⅄Ⴑ∪∨⌐♀⫯⫯⫯Ⴑ⊕⌂〉ŏ≫「⅄◡」⅄&Ⴑ♀(⌂)
　　　　　　〉꒜≫ŏ↓

「⚲|ol〉⊗〉⅄≈⳨」
♀(⌂)〉ധŏ⅄♀(¡)⠂☉↓
⊣⌐ꝋ〉꒜≫↓
「Ꮾ⫯⫯⫯⳨⅄⠂☉♦⫯⫯⫯」

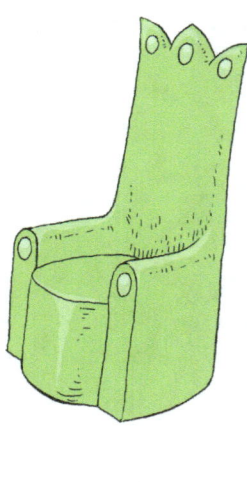

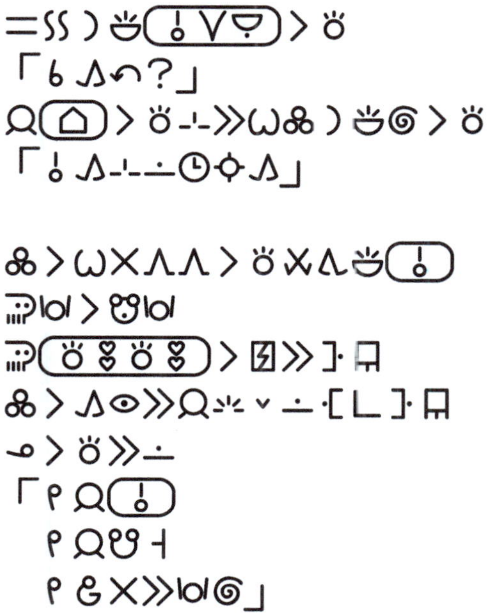

=ʃʃ) � (¡∨♡) > ŏ
「Ϭ∿⌒?」
ᘰ(⌂) > ŏ⅃-≫ꙍꙨ) profile(⊚) > ŏ
「¡∿⅃-⅃-⊙♢∿」

Ꙩ > ꙍ×∿∿ > ŏ×∿profile(¡)
⫶⊐lⲟl > Ꙙlⲟl
⫶⊐(ŏꙨŏꙨ) > 𝄞≫]·⊟
Ꙩ > ∿⊙≫ᘰ⁝ᵛ⌐[∟]·⊟
ⳋ > ŏ≫⌐
「Ϸᘰ(¡)
  ϷᘰꙞⲻ
  Ϸ⅁×≫lⲟⳗ」

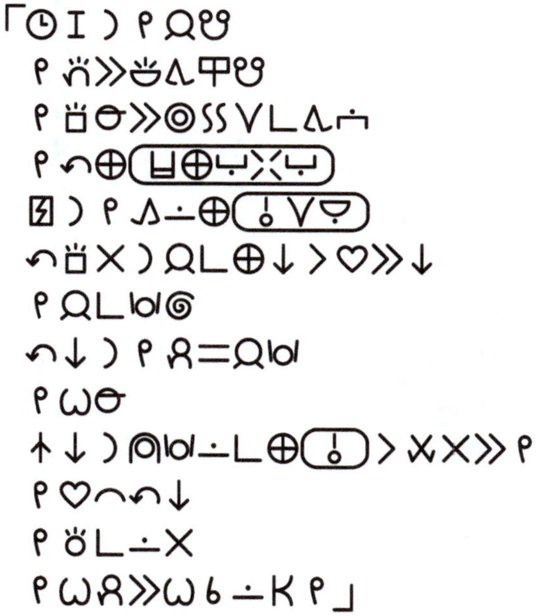

⌐⊙Ɪ⟩ᖴ♌Ꮓ
　ᖴ᷼⟫ᗘ⌁ᏋᏃ
　ᖴᴕ⊖◇⟫◎ᏕᏕᴠ⌁ᐃᴖ
　ᖴᴖ⊕⟨�375Ɏ⟩
⧅⟩ᖴᐃ÷⊕⟨⁝ᐯᏅ⟩
ᴕᴕᕽ⟩♌⌁⊕↓⟩♡⟫↓
　ᖴ♌ᒷᕽ◎
ᴕ↓⟩ᖴᏒ=♌ᕽ
　ᖴᗯᏋ
↑↓⟩ᗹᕽ÷ᒷ⊕⟨⁝⟩ᕽᕽ⟫ᖴ
　ᖴ♡ᴕ↓
　ᖴᴕᒷ÷ᕽ
　ᖴᗯᏒ⟫ᗯᑲ÷ᛕᖴ⌐

The Truth of the Mighty Person Named Oz

Dorothy's group arrived again in the Residential Land of the Blue-Green Mineral and wanted help from the important person named Oz. The Protective Person of the Large Door and many people of the city said "welcome" to Dorothy's group and heard this communication: "The Evil Woman died and became liquid, wow!" Dorothy wanted to talk to Oz at this time. But she heard this: "You must wait for several sun periods."

At the end of this time, the Person of Bird Removal could not wait and felt aggressive. "Tell this to Oz. If you do not talk to us, then Dorothy will summon the winged beasts." Oz felt afraid of the winged beasts. He could talk to the good group on the coming sun period.

On the coming sun, the group of good people went to the room of the authoritative piece of buttock furniture. But nothing was there. Like a spirit, the voice named Oz spoke: "Why did you come?" When Dorothy communicated again the group's wishes, the strange voice said: "Come back on the coming sun period."

The group did not want to keep waiting and felt aggressive towards the Oz voice. The Strong Beast roared loudly. The mammal named Toto tore the cloth wall. The group came to see a little old person in the area behind the cloth wall. He spoke the truth: "I am Oz. I am just a performance person. I do not have any strange powers."

"In the past, I was an entertainment person. I provided a voice to instruments of amusement. I know how to control large air spheres of going up. I am from the land called Omaha. By error, I arrived in the land called Oz. Because of not knowing, the people of this land felt this: I am a person of strange powers. Because of this, I acted like a powerful person. I wanted to rule. In this way, the actual powerful women of Oz did not attack me. I feel bad because of this: I spoke untruthfully. I want to grant your wishes according to my ability."

⛶|◐|∟Ω♘

⊙I)Ω(⌈⌁∀♡)⟩☼》ᔕᐱ
⊙↓)⌐⟩ᵿᔕ》⌐
#1)⌐⟩ωᵝᐸΩ∟⤬ᐱ⟩ᔕ》ᴗ⊙⌐ᑊᴄ≋
ᴗ⊙↓⟩ᑊⵝ
ᗷΩ∟⤬ᐱ⟩ᐱ❽》ᴗ⊙⌐ᑊ⟩♡◇》↓
⌈ᖴᐱⵝⵜ⌟

⊙↓)Ω(⌈⌁)⟩ωᵝᐸΩ♡⟩※》∪ᑊᗧ∟ᘻ⌐
ᴗ∪)⌐⟩ᵝ》♡∟ᄆ⌒⌒
ᘓ∟Ꝓ♡⟩ᑊᴗ
Ω♡∟※Ꝓ⟩☼》ᑊⵝ∟ᴗ♡ᑊᗧ⌐⟩♡ᴗ∞

᠉⌐♡〰 > ⅄⅋⟩⟩≈⌐ 「♡⌀⌀」
♀ > ⅄) ♀ > ♡⌀⌀
♀ > ♡∪ᗡ⅄×

ᘯ⬭⚯ᘯᚦ⌒⌒◯ ⟩ ᘯᐱ⊕ ᢒᴗ↓〓∞
↑? ⟩ ᘯ⬯ ⟩ K ᴥ≫ᘯᶟ

Powerful Knowledge of the Entertainer

In the past, the person named Oz mentioned future actions. At this time, he tried to do them. First, he wanted to give to the Person of Bird Removal and made new head innards from grain. These head innards were not real. But the Person of Bird Removal still loved the new head organ and felt this: "I became more knowledgeable."

At this time, Oz wanted to give to the Metal Person and cut a hole in the front of his body. Inside the hole, he placed a heart of soft fabric. The powder of hard plants was located inside. The Metal Person of Plant Cutting knew the falseness of the new organ of feeling, but he felt completely good.

The Beast of Fearful Feelings received a beverage of "feeling confident". When he drank it, he felt confident. He felt good because of becoming different.

The person named Dorothy wanted to go to the land called Kansas. In what way could Oz grant her wish?

⊙⋏ˇ) ◎SSⅤ >⋏⌐

⊣💩(ŏ⅋ŏ⅋) >⁓?ₔ

Ω(⌂)>Đ》💩◡◔>⋏☽》◦⁓⅋ⅤㄴΩⅢ↓

◦∞>◉》◎Ⅴ

⊙=)↶ㄴ◎SSⅤ>⋏⚡

ቀ⋏>⋏⌐

Ω☼(⊙)>⁓ω>✕ₔ

Ω(⌂)>⋏⁓⊕⌂ㄴ♡⅋

⚡

The Air Sphere of Going Up

The person named Dorothy wanted to go to the land called Kansas and waited. A good way would come. At the end of many sun periods, the person called Oz gave this wish of action: "Let's travel using a large sphere of hot air. In which direction is the land called Kansas? I do not know. But I feel this: It is located on the far side of the hot land. Me and you should go using this method."

The two of them made a large sphere of soft fabric and used a sticky substance on the inside of the sphere. In this context, the internal hot air could not go away. The two of them placed a large basket in the area below the large sphere. Oz spoke to all the people of his ruled land: "I am going to the land of a different powerful person."

In a short coming time, the large air sphere will go up. Oh, but where was the mammal named Toto? Dorothy sought her little mammal and managed to have him in a large group of many people like this: They were all watching the large sphere. At the same time, the rope of the large air sphere became broken. The transportation device went up. The knowledgeable person named Oz was inside and was gone, oh! Dorothy was still located in the Residential Land of the Blue-Green Mineral. Damn.

⊕ѱL≈X

ᘯ(⌂♡ω⊕⁘O) > ♡⌒ > KXᐃ⊕(ᵠᒡ↓≡∞)
ᘯL⋈ᐊ+ᘯ▽+ᘐᐅ > ᑏ≫♡◡

ᘯ✗L⊕⌂⧖ > ᑏ≫ᑌ◡
「ᘯ(ᘐ⊔↑ᵠᓀ) > ᘏᐅL⊕ѱ
ᒧ·L⌂ᐅᓄ) ⊕ѱL≈X > ∸」
K) ᘯ(ᘐ) > ᑌᐃᒧ·XL⊕ѱ

ᐃV↓ > K⌒⌒↓
ஃ(ᔕ▽ωᒡ∸O◎) > ∸⊕ѱ > K⌒ᐃᘯL⊕X
ᑊஃLᘯ◡ > ᐃωᐃ∸◷⟡ᐃ
「ᘯ(⌂)¦
ᑭ||| > ∸ᒧ·ᑲ」

The Hot Land of No Water

The person named Dorothy felt bad and could not go to the land called Kansas. The Person of Bird Removal and the Metal Person and the Strong Beast provided good feelings.

A battle person of the blue-green residential land gave some good knowledge: "A person named Glinda is the Powerful Woman of the Hot Land. Near her strong building, there is a hot land of no water." Maybe Glinda knew how to go to the other side of the hot land.

This big trip could be bad because of this: A group called Quadlings was located in the hot land and could be bad towards people of other lands. But the group of good people became wanting to go on the coming sun period. "Hey Dorothy! We are by your side."

ⴲⵝ

⊕⌂Ⳑ♡ⵝ❭〉Ω∭〉ⴑ≫↓
ⵕⳐⵋⴹ�ⵦⵙ⊖≫⊕⌂
ⵕ↓〉ⴷⵕⵙⳐ⊕⌂
⊣#1〉ⵦ〉ⴑⴷ⚊�⵿Ⳑⵕ⟨⌂⚸ⴑ⬧⌃O⟩
ⵕ⟨⌂⟩+ⵕⵎⵦ〉ÖⴷⵕⳐ⊕⌂
⌜ⵎⴷ
　ⵏ∞〉ⵎⵕ↓
　ⵏ⌂≫ⵎ∭Ⳑⴷ∨⌟

⸚Ⳑⵕ⟨⌂⟩〉ⴷ⊕ⴲ∨
ⴲ∨⦿〉⸛
0ⵦ〉ⴷ〉ⵝ
ⴲⵝ〉⸘≫ⵕⳐⵋⴹ

The Violent Plants

In the Residential Land of the Blue-Green Mineral, many people wanted this: The Person of Bird Removal should rule the residential land. This person became the ruling person of city. But first, he wanted to go alongside the person named Dorothy. Dorothy and her good people spoke to the people of the residential land: "We are going. You are all good because of this: You housed us travellers."

Dorothy's group went to a large plant land. There were strange large plants. Their branches moved and attacked. A violent plant seized the Person of Bird Removal.

But the Metal Person cut the branches of the plant. In a short time, a little plant seized the little mammal named Toto of little barks. The Metal Person attacked again. At this time, the group could move. "Maybe these plants protect the plant land."

The plant land was finished. At its boundary, there was a large wall of white hard material. This hard material was not strong and could become broken from just a small force. The Person of Plant Cutting used the sticks of a plant and built a device of going up. The group used it and came to see a good-looking land. All things were the same white hard material. There were small people and small animals.

⬦⌐LKⱫ

⊕˞↓)∞>ˇ>K⅄Ɽᴖ⌐lᴑˇ┤
♀⟮⌂❀ɯⴲ˞⌣◯⟯>◉»↓
ᴒˇ>⅄ꝑ»≈⅄ᴖ�∩ⴲL꤯℧ˇ
♀⟮⌂⟯>⅄)ꝑ>♡ⱳ>�∥»ㅠˇ
ȢLɯ×)∥꤯>⅄Ɽ
ᴒL≈⅄>♡⌒

The Hard Material of Breaking Possibility

In this new land, everything was little and could become broken from just a small force. The person named Dorothy saw this: A small woman obtained some white beverage from the parental bumps of a small valuable animal. When Dorothy came, the animal felt scared and kicked the small horizontal surface. As an unwanted action, the animal's leg became broken. The woman of the white beverage felt bad.

Dorothy came to know a cute different girl and a person of entertainment. The body of the entertainment person had many broken lines from damage of the past. The little cute girl was very good to Dorothy. Dorothy said this: "Please come to the land called Kansas at my side." But the girl of white hard material could not go to other lands. In other lands, she would become hard material of no movement.

The group of good people went to the other side of the land of hard material. There was a different wall. The Strong Beast gave help. The group could go up on his back. At the same time, the rear long flexible appendage of the Strong Beast damaged a small house of God. Dorothy felt good because of this: The group only slightly damaged the land of the white hard material. The Person of Bird Removal said this: "My innards are stalks of grain. Things cannot break me."

Rule of the Animals

The group of the person named Dorothy arrived in wet lowlands. There was a lot of sticky substance of the earth. Movement needed a lot of effort.

At this time, they came to be in an old large land of vegetation. The Strong Beast felt very good in the land of vegetation. "The plant land is good-looking. I feel this: I am located in my land." But the other people felt this: The plant land was dark in a bad way.

The group walked in the land of vegetation and heard many animal calls. In a short coming time, the many mammals of the plant land arrived. Reptiles and even raccoons were present.

All the animals felt love towards the Strong Beast. "Unfortunately, a large monstrous bug hunts us." The Strong Beast wanted to use his new feelings of confidence. "Let me give help. I can rule the plant land."

The Strong Beast arrived in front of the monstrous bug. This bug was large and visually disgusting, but it was asleep.

Because of this, the Strong Beast was able to defeat it using little effort. All the animals of the plant land felt good because of the death of the bug. At this time, they had a new ruling Beast.

⊕L⅋(⌒⌒▽ω⊔∴O◉)

⅋LΩ(⌂⅗ω⊕∴O) > ∴∩L♡V |||

∧∺ > ω≫⌀ |||

⅋(X⊗X⌀+) > ⊙ > ∧≫∩V

Ω◉↓) ⊔⊖ > K∧V

↑↓) ∽ > K⋇⊞⊖

ΩL⋉⩲+⫶?⊖ > ⊕∧∺

⊢Ω⋇(X) > ⋇≫∽|| > ⊔≫∽||∧⅃∩

⅋(X) > ⌀∣∩

∽↓)Ω(⌂) > ⊞⊓⊖L♡⅗ > ∧≫⫶?Ω⅗

⫶?⅋ > ∧⅍≫⅋⌣ > ∧∺ > ∧≫∽∧⊔∙✕∩

⊙↓)⅋LΩ⌣ > ∴⊕⅜L⅋(⌒⌒) > ♡♡⌣

⊕⧖⟩⅋⟩ᗅ⌂1
�||Lɒ⟨ss⟩⟩ᒪ≫ᑌ
ᒪ⟩ⵎ≫ᛉ⏝ᗅ⅋Lᗅ⋁

ᗉ⟨⌂⟩⟩ⲱⵎ
「⌂ⵡᒪᗉⵡ⏝⟨ⵆⵡↄ⏁ⵡᛎⵡ⟩⸱?」
「ⵆⵡ⌂ⵕ⟩⸱ⵡ」
ᗉ⏝Lɒ⟨ss⟩⟩ⵎ≫ⵡ̈Lↄⵡ

☉ⵡ⌄⟩⅋Lᗉ⏝⟩ⵡ⌂ⵡLᗉ⟨ⵆ⟩
ᑌⵡ�727Lⵡ⁼⟩⸱ᑌ⟩ⵆ≫ⲱLᗉ⟨⌂⟩⟩ᒪ≫ᑌ
「ⵡ⏝」

The Land of the Group Called Quadlings

The group of the person named Dorothy was located at a hill of many large stones. Upward movement needed a lot of energy. The group called Hammer-Heads was watching and protected the large hill. Regarding these strange people, the lower part of the head could become long. In this way, they could attack using their heads. The Person of Bird Removal and the ruling Beast tried to go upwards. But the violent people called Hammer-Heads struck the two of them and lowered them both to the foot of the hill.

The Hammer-Heads were powerful in a bad way. Because of this, Dorothy used the headdress of yellow metal and summoned the winged humanlike beasts. The winged beasts successfully carried the good group and moved upwards and transported them to the other side of the hill. At this time, the group of good people were located in the red land of the Quadlings and felt good.

In the grain land, the group went to one house. Two love people of the group called Quadlings opened the door. The woman gave good food to the travel group.

Dorothy wanted to know: "Where is the strong building of the Good Powerful Woman called Glinda located?" "Oh, her building is near." The good people of the Quadling community gave knowledge of the way to go.

In a short coming time, the group of good people went to the strong building of Glinda. Many protective people with the same clothing were at the door and heard the wishes of Dorothy and opened the door. "Welcome."

ႶⅠଠⅠ◡ ⟨ 𝟤 ⊔ ↑ ♀ ᵕ⟩

𝟪 › ◡ ⟫ 𝍫 ⌒

Ⴍ ⟨⌂ ⅋ ⱳ ⊕ ⌒⌒ ◯⟩ › ≈ ⟫ ⌉⸳ ⌒

⌒ › ⋀ ⌂ ∟ ⌒ ◡ ⟨𝟤⟩

Ⴍ ⟨𝟤⟩ › ◡ ⦿ › ⋀ ⊥ 𝝅 ⦂ ⌊ ♡ ⅋ › 𝟨 ⟫ ◡ ⊙ ⅋ ⟫ 𝌐 ⌒⌒ △

Ⴍ ⟨⌂⟩ › ŏ ⟫ 𝟠 ⋁ ◡ ⌊ ⊙ Ⅰ

「 ⊙ ↓ ⟩ ⌿ ⱳ ⋀ ⊕ ⟨ ♀ ⩊ ↓ ⚌ ∞ ⟩ 」

ႶⅠଠⅠ ⟨𝟤⟩ › ⱳ ⏨ ⟫ ◡

↑ Ⴍ ⟨⌂⟩ ᵕ ⏨ ⟫ 𝌐 ⊖ ⌊ ଠⅠ 𝟨 ⌒ ⋀ Ⴍ ⟨𝟤⟩

Ⴍ ⟨⌂⟩ › ⏨

♁⬭>Ɛ≫ﷺ(ŏ℘ŏ℘)
　　　>ŏⱽ≫⸳⎡∟⊞⊩1⨪⊞⊩✕⨪☉||1
⎡ℙ⸳⸸⋀⌂ℙ⎦
☉ⱽ)ƧƧ∟ⱶ◎>⋀≫ᵔ
⊞⊩>⋏✕

The Good Powerful Woman Named Glinda

The group improved their outer appearance. The person named Dorothy used water on her face. They went to the building of the Good Woman named Glinda. Glinda was good-looking and stayed on butt furniture of red mineral and had red hair and a white cute outfit. Dorothy communicated her great actions of the past. "At this time, I want to go to the land called Kansas."

The Powerful Woman named Glinda wanted to give help. But Dorothy should give the headdress of strange powers to Glinda. Dorothy gave.

Glinda spoke: "In the future, I will do this: The winged beasts should transport the Person of Bird Removal to the Residential Land of the Blue-Green Mineral. He should become their ruling person. The Metal Person should go to the land of the group called Winkies. He should rule them. The ruling Beast should go to the old plant land. He should rule it. When these three things are finished, I should give the powerful headdress to the winged beasts. Other beings should not rule the winged beasts."

Glinda continued to speak: "O Dorothy! Your footwear of white metal is strangely powerful. If you use it, you can go to any land using three foot movements."

All people and all animals were very emotional and said "goodbye". Dorothy held the mammal named Toto and caused the back of one item of footwear to make a small noise against the other item of footwear three times. "Let me go to my home." In a short time, a wind of strange powers transported her. The footwear became gone.

Ah, Home!

Again, the person named Dorothy was located in the land called Kansas. She felt very good and saw this: The caretaker named Henry had built a new house in the grain land. With intensity, Dorothy moved towards both arms of the caretaker named Em. "In the past, I was in the land called Oz. I have come back in my home! Ah!" Again the parental group was united. Dorothy felt good.

www.ingramcontent.com/pod-product-compliance
Lightning Source LLC
Chambersburg PA
CBHW051840020726
47502CB00005B/1883